THE FASCINATING FOOTBALLER

LIFE LESSONS

By Michael Caleb Likambi

Books by the author:

Tammy and The Shipwreck
Softback: ISBN-13: 978-1-913266-07-3
Rags to Riches
Softback: ISBN-13: 978-1-913266-11-0
The Dreamer
Softback: ISBN-13 978-1-913266-12-7
Wartime
Softback: ISBN-13 978-1-913266-19-6
The Stepbrothers
Softback: ISBN-13 978-1-913266-18-9
The Run for Gold
Softback: ISBN-13: 978-1-913266-22-6
The Fascinating Footballer
Softback: ISBN-13: 978-1-913266-28-8
The Football Prodigy
Softback: ISBN-13: 978-1-913266-29-5
Hunger for Fame
Softback: ISBN-13: 978-1-913266-30-1

Books by Michael Caleb Likambi:

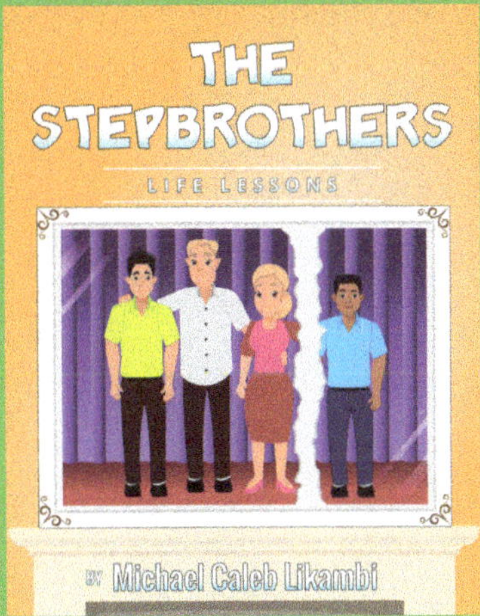

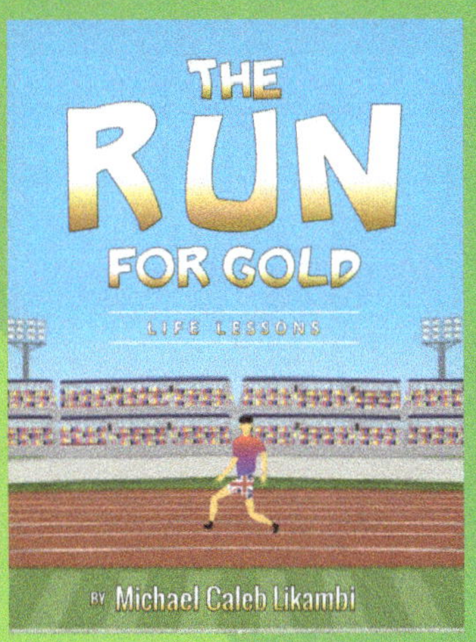

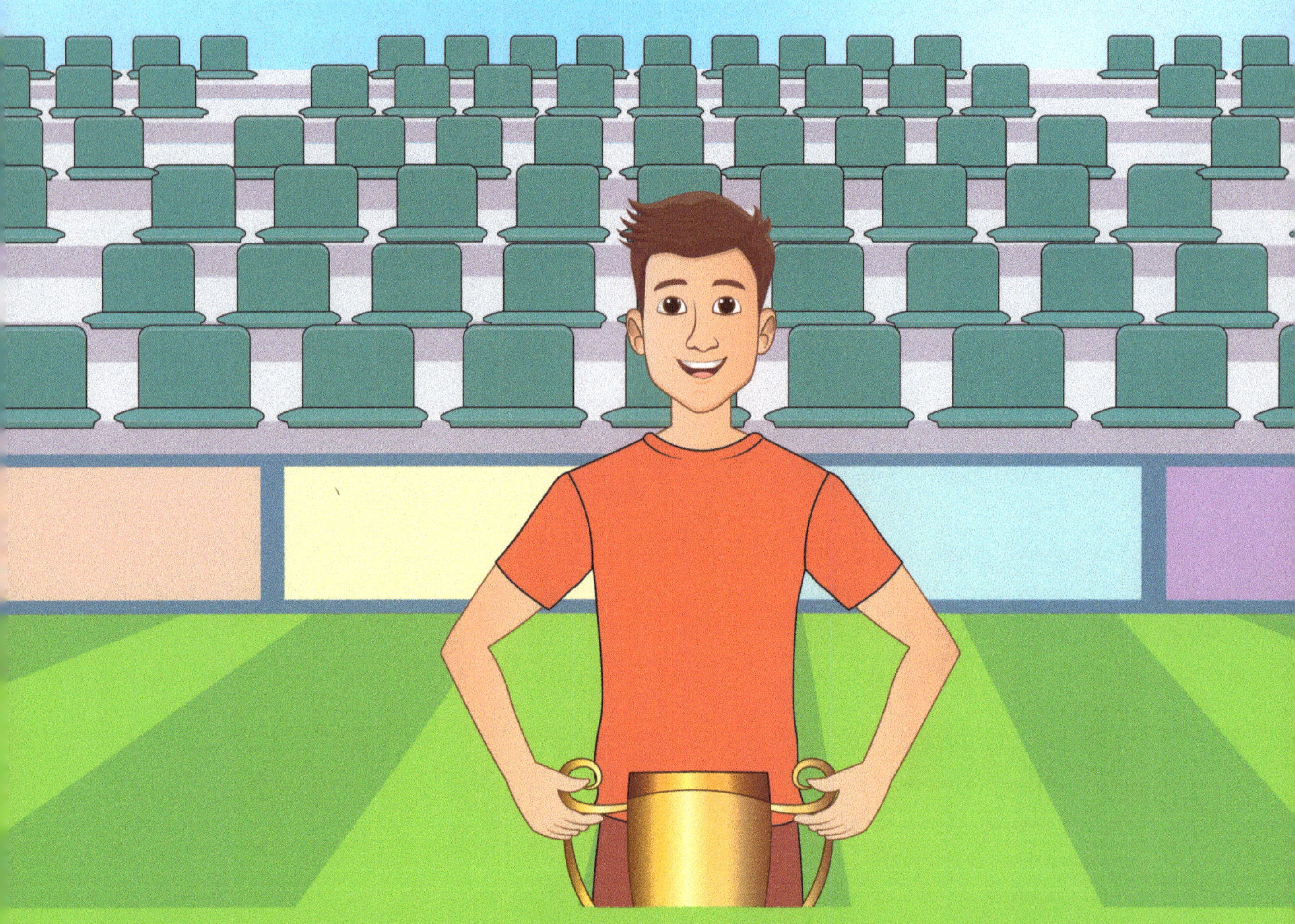

There once was a young boy named James Stirrup, who was very well-known for his outstanding football skills. He was the best player on his team.

Things were going well for James, and they kept on getting better and better for him as his skills were growing and he was attracting more attention from bigger clubs.

One day, James was called up for a match and he was told there would be many scouts willing to give young players like him a contract.

You impressed me today.

CONTRACT

Appointment and duration

2.1 The Club engages the Player as a professional footballer on the terms and conditions of this contract and subject to the Rules.

2.2 This contract shall remain in force until the date specified in clause 2 of Schedule 2 hereto subject to any earlier determination pursuant to the terms of this contract.

3. Duties and Obligations of the Player

3.1 The Player agrees:

3.1.1 when directed by an authorised official of the Club:

3.1.1.1 to attend matches in which the Club is engaged;

3.1.1.2 to participate in any matches in which he is selected to play for the Club; and

3.1.1.3 to attend at any reasonable place for the purposes of and to participate in training and match preparation;

3.1.2 to play to the best of his skill and ability at all times;

3.1.3 except to the extent prevented by injury or illness to maintain a high standard of physical fitness at all times and not to indulge in any activity sport or practice which might endanger such fitness or inhibit his mental or physical ability to play practice or train;

3.1.4 to undertake such other duties and to participate in such other activities as are consistent with the performance of his duties under clauses 3.1.1 to 3.1.3 and as are reasonably required of the Player;

4

3.1.5 that he has given all necessary authorities for the release to the Club of his medical records and will continue to make the same available as requested by the Club from time to time during the continuance of this contract;

3.1.6 to comply with and act in accordance with all lawful instructions of any authorised official of the Club;

3.1.7 to play football solely for the Club or as authorised by the Club or as required by the Rules;

James Stirrup

3.1.8 to observe the Laws of the Game when playing football;

3.1.9 to observe the Rules but in the case of the Club Rules to the extent only that they do not conflict with or seek to vary the express terms of this contract;

3.1.10 to submit promptly to such medical and dental examinations as the Club may reasonably require and to undergo at no expense to himself such treatment as may be

Signature '....................

Throughout the match, he was able to amaze all the scouts and was given trials.

CONTRACT

Appointment and duration

2.1 The Club engages the Player as a professional footballer on the terms and conditions of this contract and subject to the Rules.

2.2 This contract shall remain in force until the date specified in clause 2 of Schedule 2 hereto subject to any earlier determination pursuant to the terms of this contract.

3. Duties and Obligations of the Player

3.1 The Player agrees:

3.1.1 when directed by an authorised official of the Club:

3.1.1.1 to attend matches in which the Club is engaged;

3.1.1.2 to participate in any matches in which he is selected to play for the Club; and

3.1.1.3 to attend at any reasonable place for the purposes of and to participate in training and match preparation;

3.1.2 to play to the best of his skill and ability at all times;

3.1.3 except to the extent prevented by injury or illness to maintain a high standard of physical fitness at all times and not to indulge in any activity sport or practice which might endanger such fitness or inhibit his mental or physical ability to play practise or train;

3.1.4 to undertake such other duties and to participate in such other activities as are consistent with the performance of his duties under clauses 3.1.1 to 3.1.3 and as are reasonably required of the Player;

4

3.1.5 that he has given all necessary authorities for the release to the Club of his medical records and will continue to make the same available as requested by the Club from time to time during the continuance of this contract;

3.1.6 to comply with and act in accordance with all lawful instructions of any authorised official of the Club;

3.1.7 to play football solely for the Club or as authorised by the Club or as required by the Rules;

James Stirrup

3.1.8 to observe the Laws of the Game when playing football;

3.1.9 to observe the Rules but in the case of the Club Rules to the extent only that they do not conflict with or seek to vary the express terms of this contract;

3.1.10 to submit promptly to such medical and dental examinations as the Club may reasonably require and to undergo at no expense to himself such treatment as may be

Signature'...............

On James's big match to determine his spot in the team, disaster struck. The ball rolled towards the centre of the pitch, and everyone ran towards the ball. James got to the ball first, but people were still rushing towards him and then someone slid in and bent his knee back.

AHHH !

James screamed in agony, as he could not bear the pain and everything went black. He was on the side of the pitch but when he tried to get up, his leg just gave up on him. Little did James know that this would be a moment that would change his life.

HELP!

After the match, James was taken to the hospital to get a checkup on his leg, and he was given a pair of crutches and a leg cast. Over the course of a few days, James didn't think much of his injury, but it had played a crucial role in his life.

HOSPITA
ENTRANCE

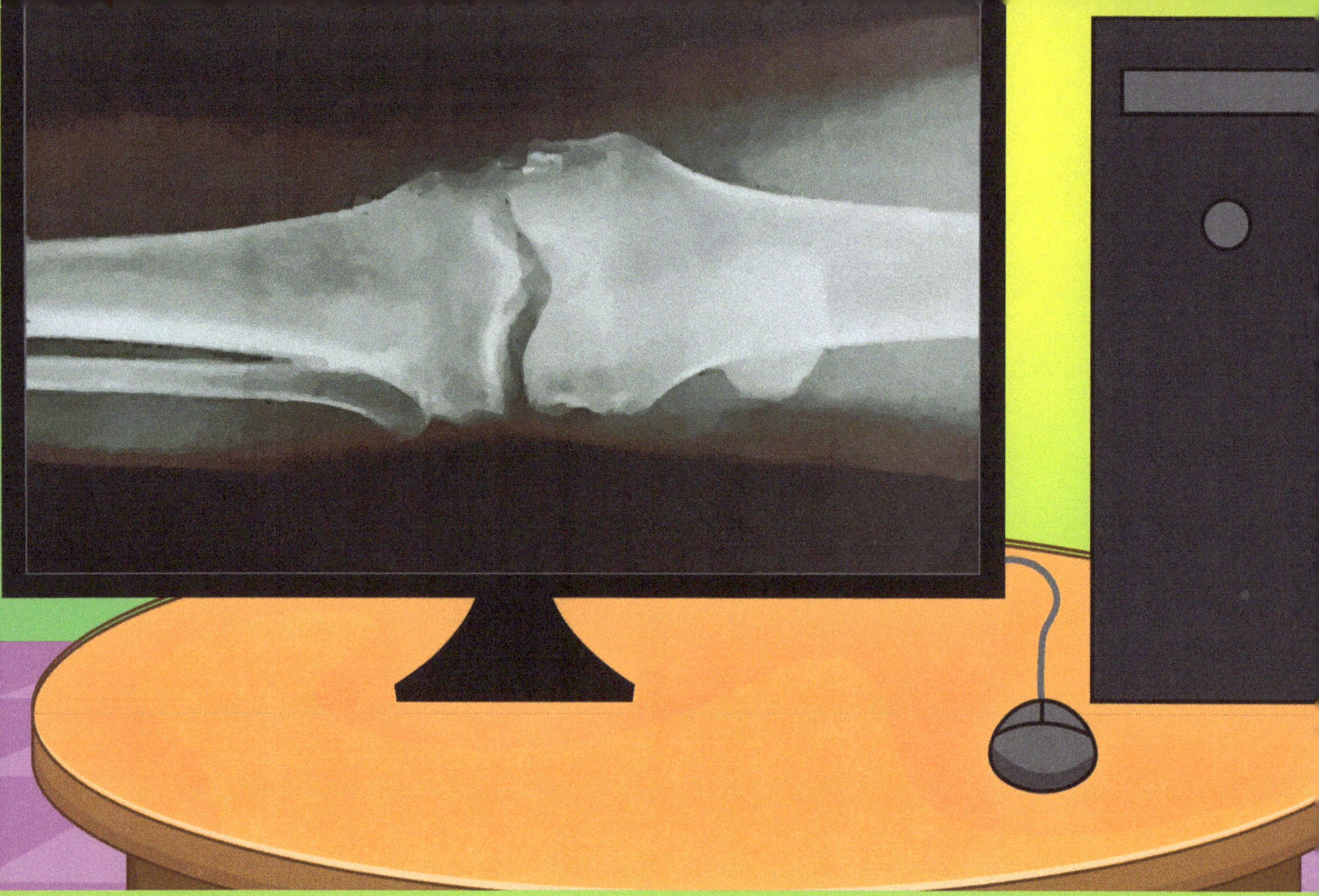

While they were at home one day, a letter came in the mailalerting James' family about their next appointment. So they got ready and went. When they got to the hospital they sat in the queue and waited until they were called. When James and his parents got the X-ray back it showed that James had ruptured one of the ligaments in his knee and that he would not play football again. They also told him that he would need surgery, but he would have to wait a few years because he was too young.

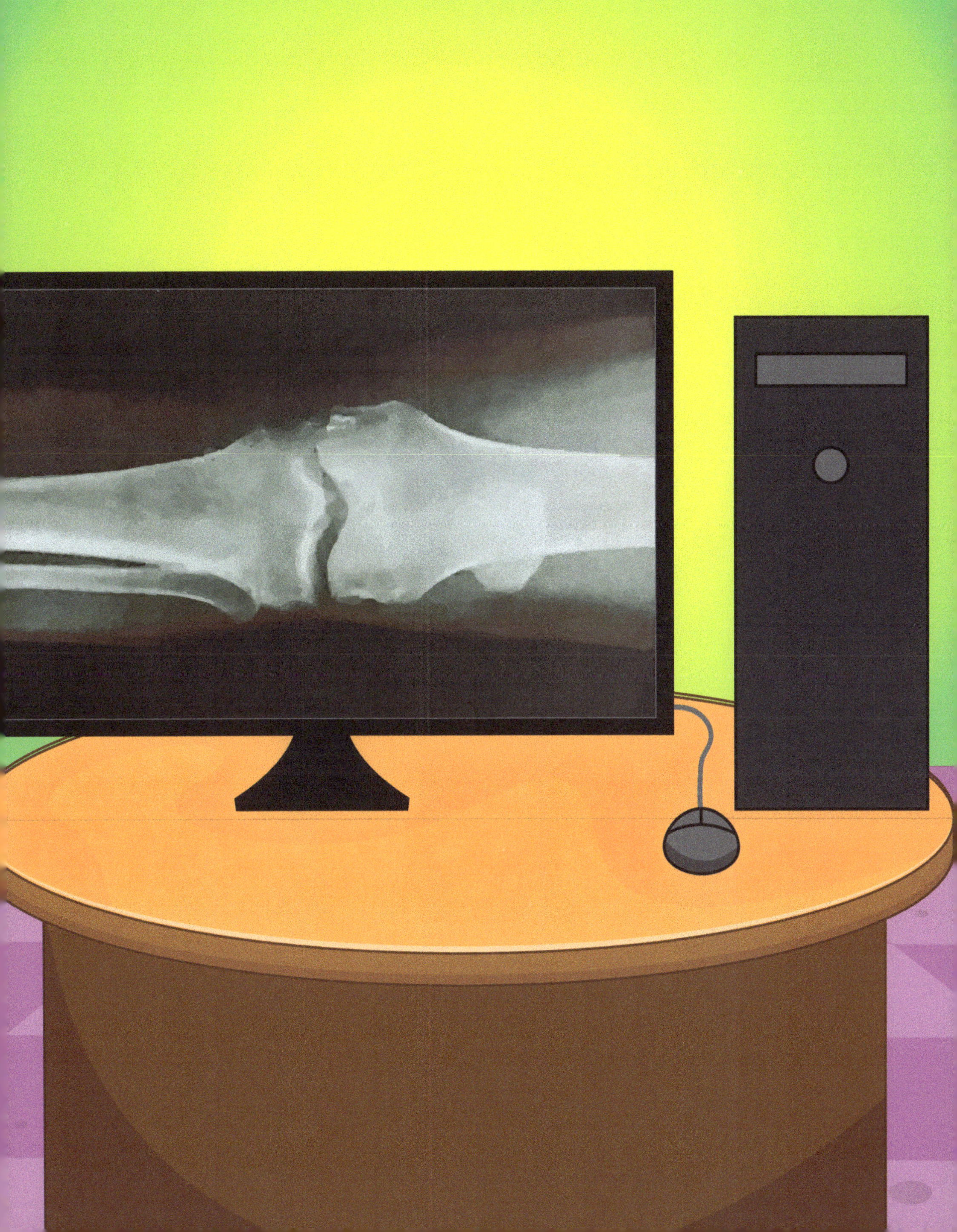

James's parents did not want their son to have surgery, since they believed James could heal naturally. All this news broke James' heart and the thought of never playing football again caused him to simply break down.

Over time, James managed to adapt to this new way of life, despite how deeply it upset him. Soon, James started to give up all hope of ever recovering and returning to play football again. When his parents realised how down he was, they decided to give him hope.

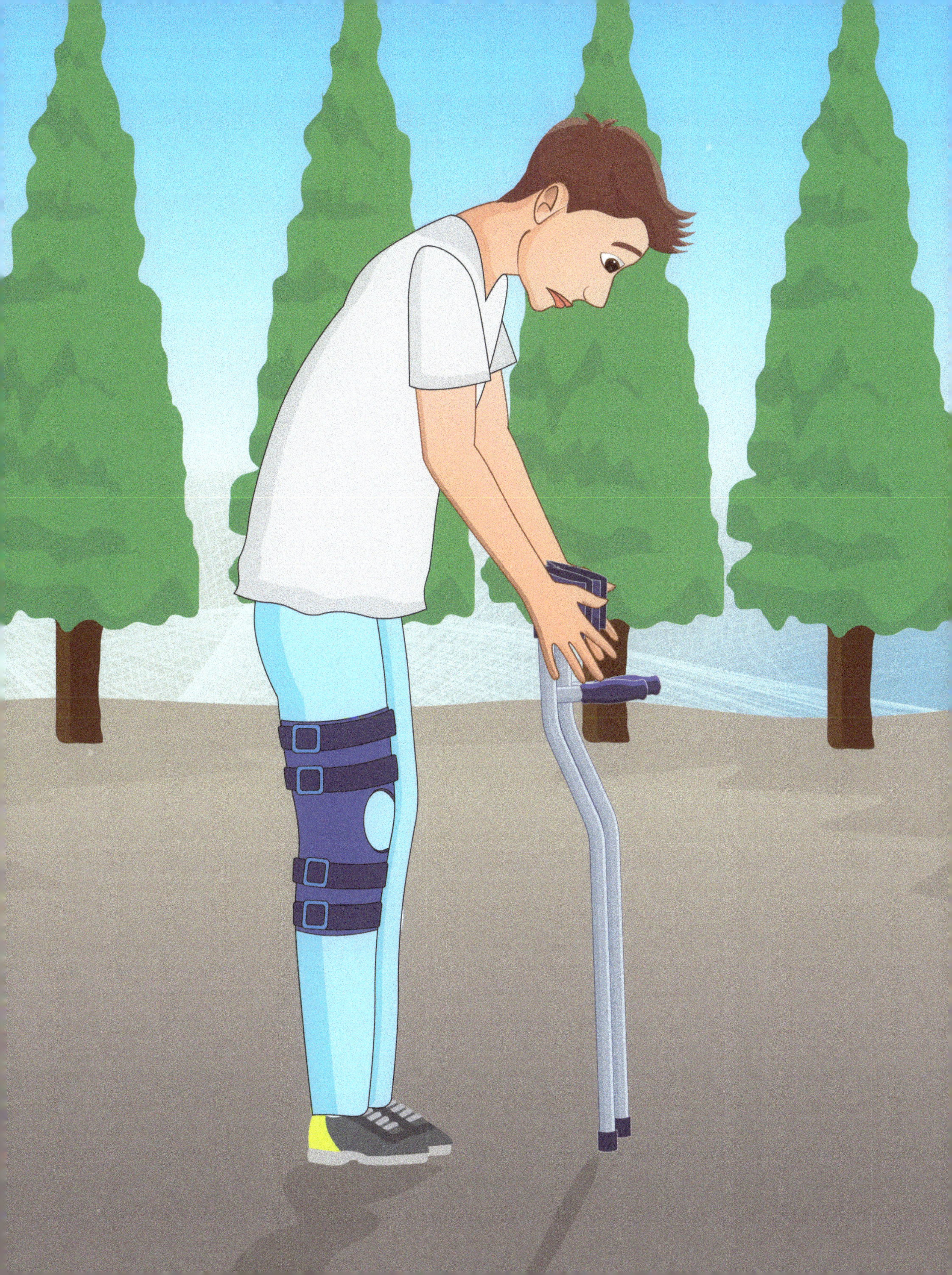

His parents knew that James had strong willpower and belief, and that anything he put his mind to he could achieve. They decided they would make James believe he had had the surgery and after weeks of planning it was arranged that they would meet up at the hospital.

Be quick, James!
We have
an appointment.

On the big day, James and his family got ready to leave and out of all of them, James was the most excited. He already believed he was going to be healed and could not wait. When they arrived, James was put to sleep, and everyone waited for him to wake up. When he did, everyone was glad to see how happy James looked and it spread a smile to everyone in the room.

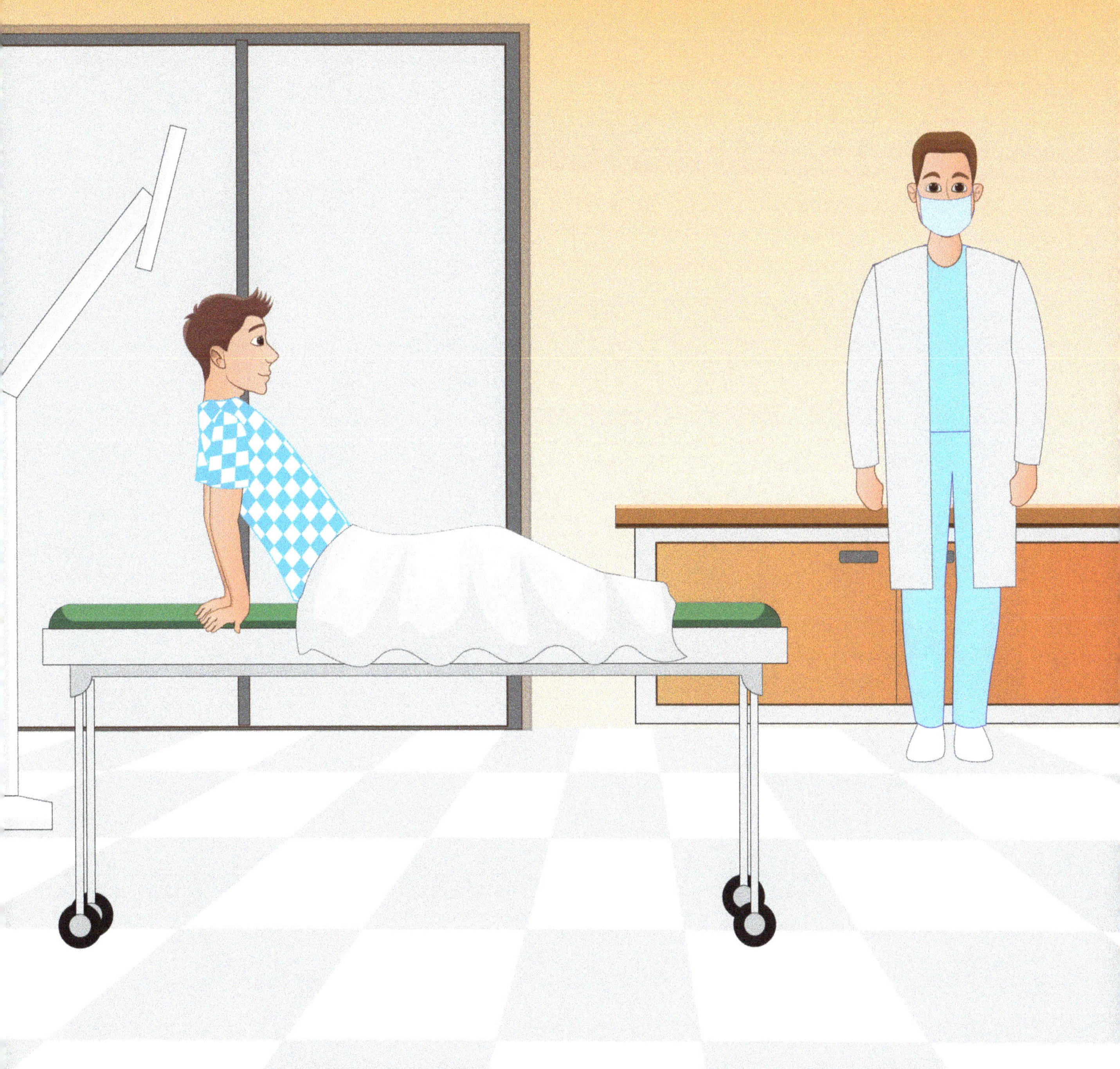
URGERY ROOM

Over time, everyone started to notice changes in James's health as he became more active and happier and soon, he was able to get rid of his crutches and was walking then he started to progress from one stage to another and soon he was able to jog and from there on he just kept on getting better and better just because he believed in himself that he was healed.

Hospital

Appointment

Lorem ipsum dolor sit amet, consectetuer adipiscing elit, sed diam nonummy nibh euismod tincidunt ut laoreet dolore magna aliquam erat volutpat. Ut wisi enim ad minim veniam, quis nostrud exerci tation ullamcorper suscipit lobortis nisl ut.

Lorem ipsum dolor sit amet, consectetuer adipiscing elit, sed diam nonummy nibh euismod tincidunt ut laoreet dolore magna aliquam erat volutpat. Ut wisi enim ad minim veniam, quis nostrud exerci tation ullamcorper suscipit lobortis nisl ut Lorem ipsum dolor sit amet, consectetuer adipiscing elit, sed diam nonummy nibh euismod tincidunt ut laoreet dolore magna aliquam erat volutpat. Ut wisi enim ad minim veniam, quis nostrud exerci tation ullamcorper suscipit lobortis nisl ut Lorem ipsum dolor sit amet, consectetuer adipiscing elit, sed diam nonummy nibh euismod tincidunt ut laoreet dolore magna aliquam erat volutpat. Ut wisi enim ad minim veniam, quis nostrud exerci tation ullamcorper suscipit lobortis nisl ut Lorem ipsum dolor sit amet, consectetuer adipiscing elit, sed diam nonummy nibh euismod tincidunt ut laoreet dolore magna aliquam erat volutpat. Ut wisi enim ad minim veniam, quis nostrud exerci tation ullamcorper suscipit lobortis nisl ut.

Scan conditions

- *Lorem ipsum dolor sit amet, consectetuer adipiscing elit, sed diam nonummy.*

Although James was progressing extremely fast, he still had to take things easy so he would occasionally go back to the hospital for checkups. The doctors were amazed by his progress, but he had to have another scan soon.

Hospital

Appointment

Lorem ipsum dolor sit amet, consectetuer adipiscing elit, sed diam nonummy nibh euismod tincidunt ut laoreet dolore magna aliquam erat volutpat. Ut wisi enim ad minim veniam, quis nostrud exerci tation ullamcorper suscipit lobortis nisl ut

Lorem ipsum dolor sit amet, consectetuer adipiscing elit, sed diam nonummy nibh euismod tincidunt ut laoreet dolore magna aliquam erat volutpat. Ut wisi enim ad minim veniam, quis nostrud exerci tation ullamcorper suscipit lobortis nisl ut Lorem ipsum dolor sit amet, consectetuer adipiscing elit, sed diam nonummy nibh euismod tincidunt ut laoreet dolore magna aliquam erat volutpat. Ut wisi enim ad minim veniam, quis nostrud exerci tation ullamcorper suscipit lobortis nisl ut Lorem ipsum dolor sit amet, consectetuer adipiscing elit, sed diam nonummy nibh euismod tincidunt ut laoreet dolore magna aliquam erat volutpat. Ut wisi enim ad minim veniam, quis nostrud exerci tation ullamcorper suscipit lobortis nisl ut Lorem ipsum dolor sit amet, consectetuer adipiscing elit, sed diam nonummy nibh euismod tincidunt ut laoreet dolore magna aliquam erat volutpat. Ut wisi enim ad minim veniam, quis nostrud exerci tation ullamcorper suscipit lobortis nisl ut

Scan conditions

- Lorem ipsum dolor sit amet, consectetuer adipiscing elit, sed diam nonummy
- Lorem ipsum dolor sit amet, consectetuer adipiscing elit, sed diam nonummy nibh euismod tincidunt

  Lorem ipsum dolor sit amet, consectetuer adipiscing elit,

- Lorem ipsum dolor sit amet, consectetuer adipiscing elit,
- Lorem ipsum dolor sit amet,
- Lorem ipsum dolor sit amet, consectetuer adipiscing elit, sed diam nonummy nibh euismod tincidunt

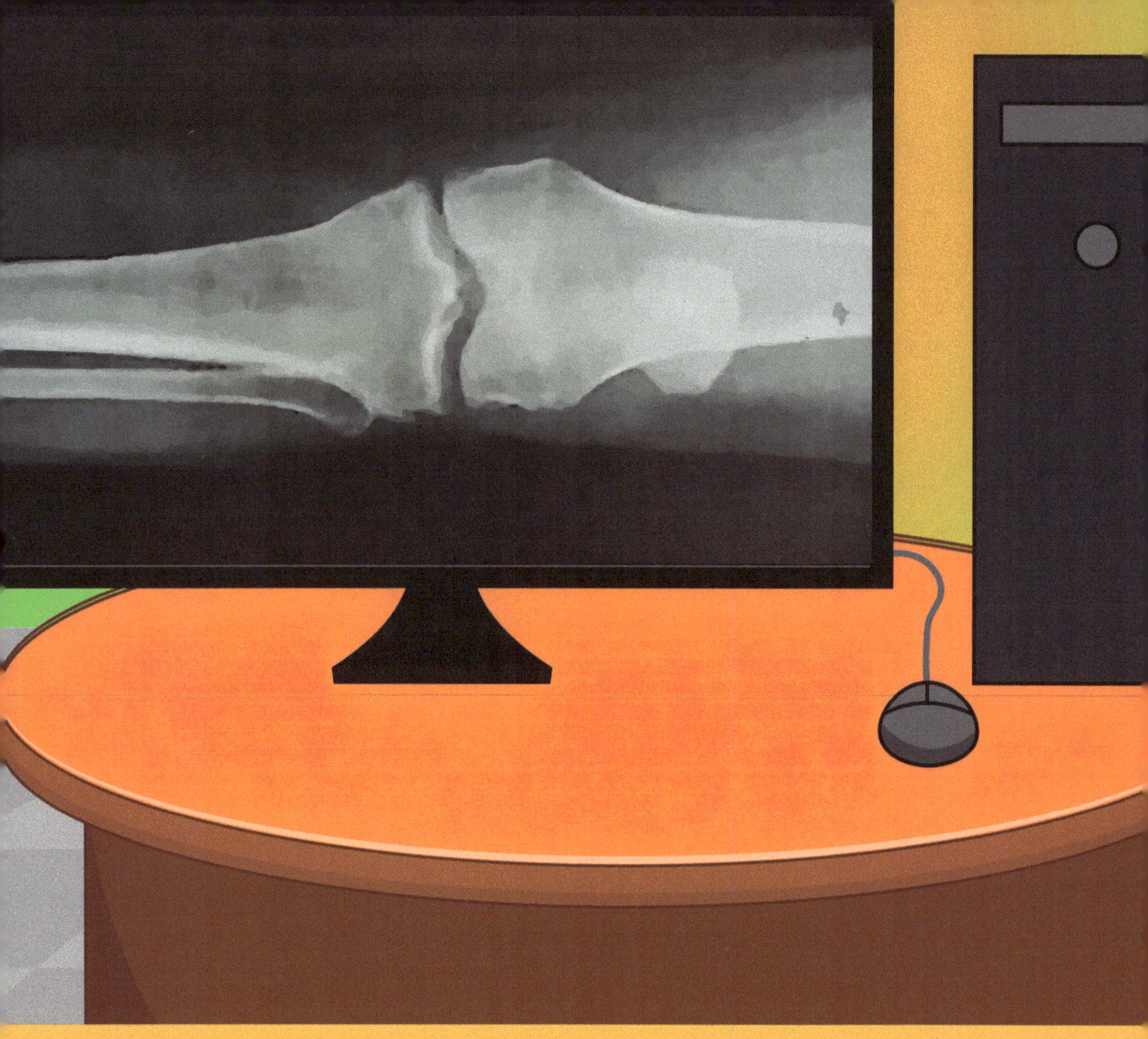

When the doctors got the result back from the second scan, they were amazed at just how much he had really healed and predicted he would only need six more months to recover rather than two years and this is all because he believed he could do it.

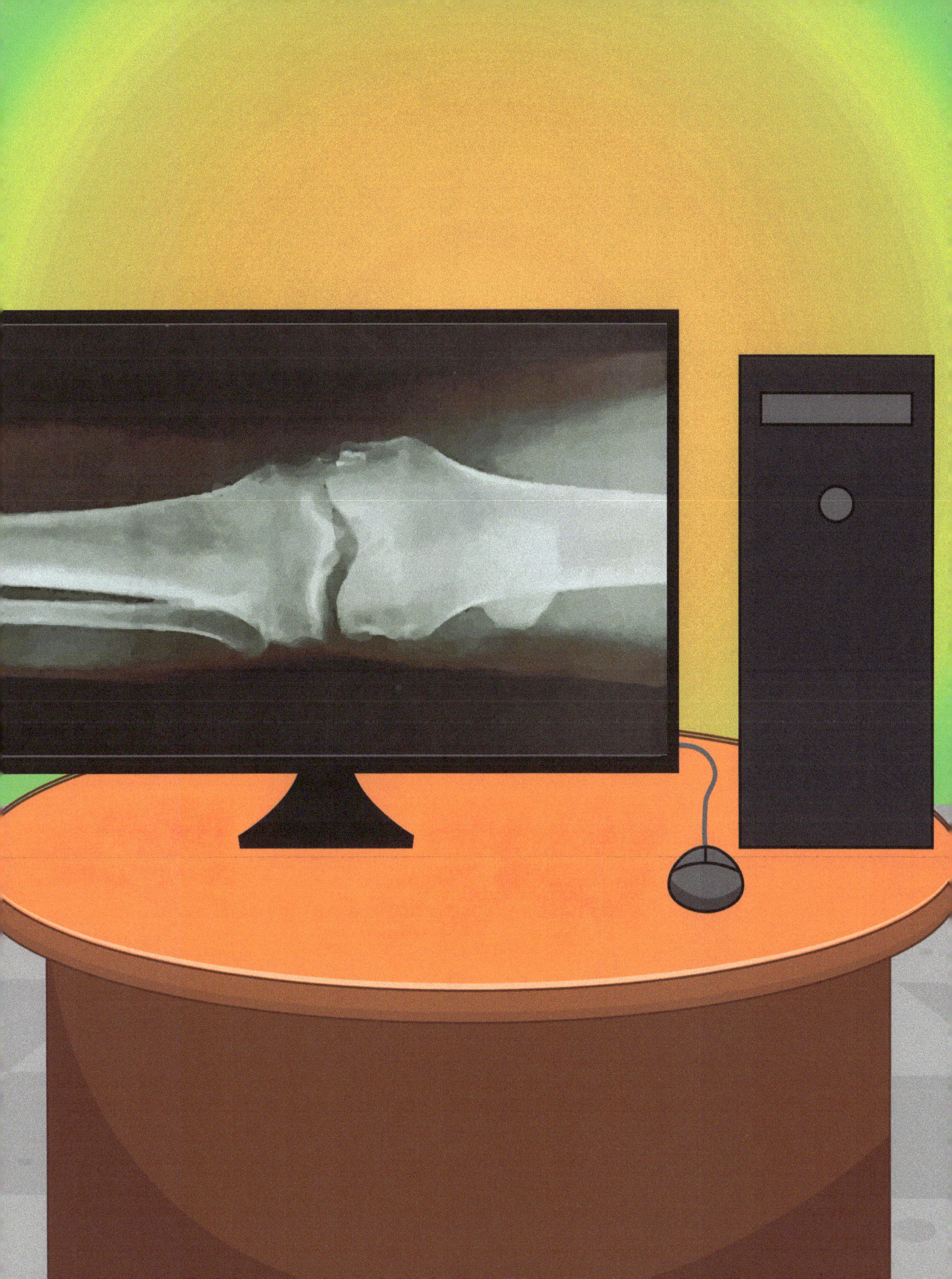

James was soon able to go back to what he loved most: football.

The end!

ABOUT THE AUTHOR

MICHAEL CALEB LIKAMBI

"Always surround yourself with people who inspire you to be great, but most importantly, be that person who inspires others to be great." Caleb Likambi

Caleb Likambi is no ordinary teenager. Coming from a family of talented young writers, Michael Caleb Likambi debuted as an author at the age of 12 with his best-selling book, Tammy and the Shipwreck, and in less than a year, he had published five books. Now, at just 14, he represents a beacon of inspiration for aspiring young authors globally. Caleb's journey into the world of writing began as a way to express his vivid imagination and share valuable life lessons with his peers. With six books under his belt and these three new releases, he follows in his little sister's footsteps (who debuted as an author at the tender age of five and by the age of eight, had published nine books), and continues to prove that age is no barrier to creativity and accomplishment. In addition, In August 2023, Caleb wrote and illustrated 10 new books in his life lessons series, three of which are currently being released, with the remaining seven to be released next year.

Caleb is an ultra-confident and grounded young man, whose kind, caring, compassionate, and humble personality makes him a true leader and friend to everyone—always standing up for those who are bullied or mistreated. He is a positive role model for children and young people all across the globe.

He has been the Head Boy at his secondary school for three consecutive years and has been on the School Council numerous times throughout his time in primary school. He is also a gifted and natural sportsman, who has won numerous trophies and awards, both as an individual and for his primary and secondary schools.

ABOUT THE AUTHOR

MICHAEL CALEB LIKAMBI

"Reading is such fun. It has the power to expand your imagination and take you into different parts and cultures of the world at the same time."
Caleb Likambi

.Caleb's genuine passion for reading and learning is second to none, which goes back to his childhood when he would read until he fell asleep. He's read over 800 books to date and never stops requesting new books. He has been interviewed by and featured on diverse media platforms, including BBC Radio Merseyside and the Liverpool Echo.

Caleb's dedication to sharing his love of reading and writing extends beyond his own books. Together with his siblings, he actively advocates for literacy and education, speaking in schools, libraries, and events and working to make diverse children books accessible to children from all backgrounds. Through his donations to schools, young people, and libraries, Caleb hopes to inspire young readers to discover the joy and transformative power of reading. He was the winner of the BBI Young Leader of the Year Award 2024.

With his latest releases, he continues to inspire the younger generation with relatable characters and powerful messages, encouraging readers to dream big, overcome obstacles, and embrace their unique gifts and talents.

Get Your Autographed Copies & Invite Caleb at Your School, Library, or Event
Caleb Likambi's latest books are a great addition to your library and inspirational children books collection. Whether you're a young reader, a parent, an educator, or a book enthusiast, Caleb's stories will leave a lasting impression.

For press inquiries, interviews, copies of the books, or event bookings, please contact:
Likambi Global Publishing Ltd
Email: enquiries@likambiglobalpublishing.com
Phone: +44 (0) 7539216072
Website: www.likambiglobalpublishing.com

ABOUT THE PUBLISHER

LIKAMBI GLOBAL PUBLISHING

Published by Likambi Global Publishing Ltd.
Email: publishing@likambiglobalpublishing.com
Tel: +44 (0) 7539 216072
www.likambiglobalpublishing.com

We are a Dynamic Family-Led Cutting-Edge Global Publisher set up to simplify and enhance your writing and publishing experience and unique journey to becoming a renowned and confident author.

Whether you are an adult or child, we have a special team that is devoted to working with you throughout your writing and publishing journey with us! All of our consultants and coaches/mentors are bestselling authors with years of hands-on experience and a wealth of knowledge uniquely tailored to meet your individual needs!

Our goal is to provide you with the ultimate writing and publishing experience required to share your unique message and voice as an author with the world and strive to greater heights!

Publications are done three times a year; January, June, and November. All manuscripts must be received at least 90 days prior to publication dates.

OTHER CHILDREN BOOKS BY LIKAMBI GLOBAL PUBLISHING

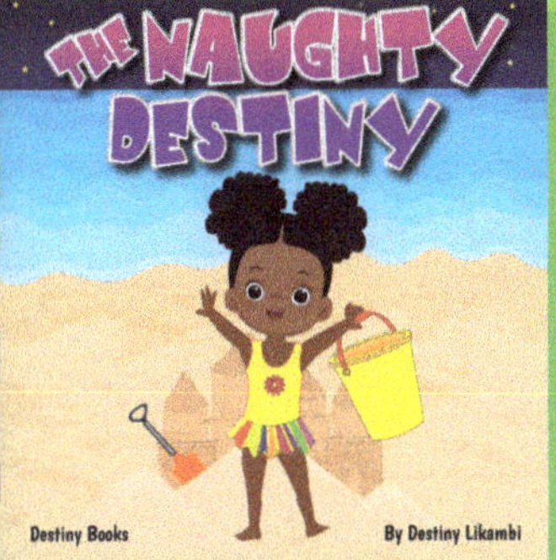

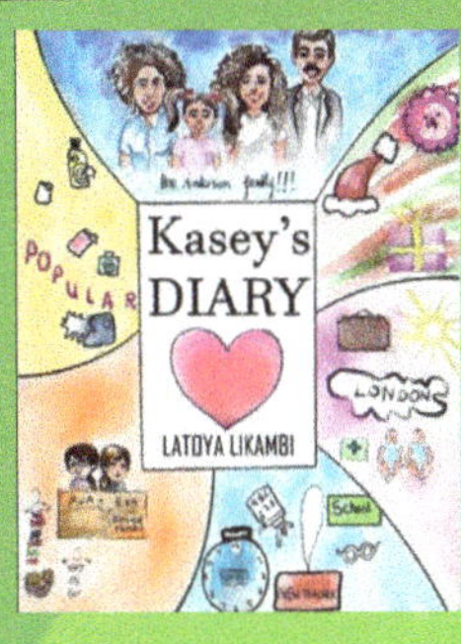

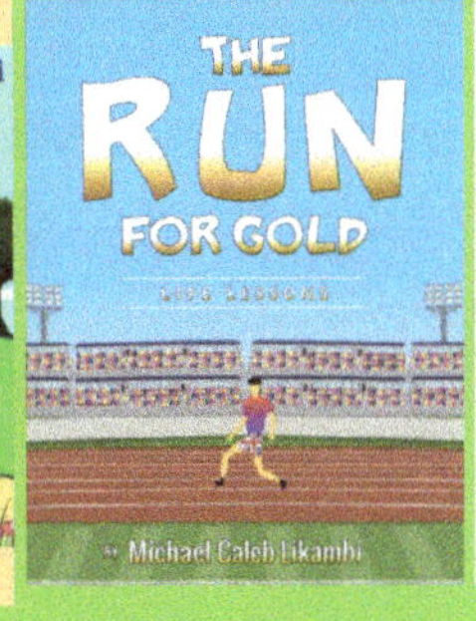

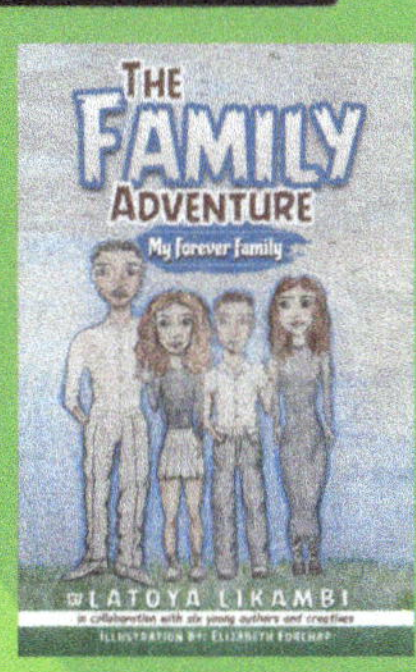
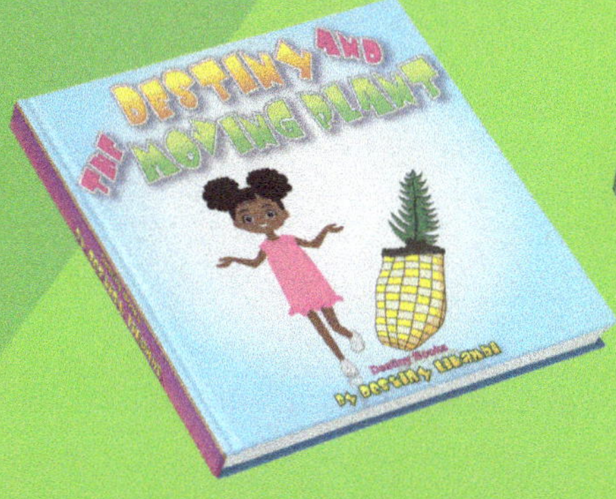

OTHER CHILDREN BOOKS BY LIKAMBI GLOBAL PUBLISHING

Allie and the Creepy Forest.
Softback: ISBN-13 978-1-913266-23-3

The New Shoe.
Softback: ISBN-13 978-1-913266-24-0

The Stepbrothers
Softback: ISBN-13 978-1-913266-18-9

Rags to Riches
Softback: ISBN-13: 978-1-913266-11-0

The Dreamer
Softback: ISBN-13 978-1-913266-12-7

The Naughty Destiny
Softback: ISBN-13: 978-1-913266-13-4

Destiny and The Troll
 Hardback ISBN 13: 978-1-913266-06-6
 Softback ISBN 13: 978-1-913266-05-9

The Girl on The Journey
 Hardback ISBN 13: 978-1-913266-93-6
 Softback ISBN 13: 978-1-913266-94-3

Tammy and the Shipwreck
 Softback ISBN 13: 978-1-913266-07-3

Short Stories by Latoya Likambi
 Softback ISBN 13: 978-1-913266-03-5

Destiny and the Moving Plant.
Softback: ISBN-13 978-1-913266-25-7

Kasey's Diary
 Hardback ISBN 13: 978-1-093291-26-1
 Softback ISBN 13: 978-0-368630-50-7

The Snow Sisters
Softback: ISBN-13 978-1-913266-14-1

Wartime
Softback: ISBN-13 978-1-913266-19-6

Chicky and the Forest
Softback: ISBN-13 978-1-913266-15-8

The Summer Holiday
Softback: ISBN-13 978-1-913266-21-9

The Run for Gold
Softback: ISBN-13: 978-1-913266-22-6

Family Adventure
Softback ISBN 13: 978-1-913266-23-3

Anderson Adventure (Kasey's Diary Book 2)
 Softback ISBN 13: 978-1-913266-99-8

The Babysitter
Softback ISBN-13: 978-1913266974

www.ingramcontent.com/pod-product-compliance
Lightning Source LLC
Chambersburg PA
CBHW042108160726
48295CB00017B/1021